SUMMER IN CIMARRON & LUNCH AT THE DIXIE DINER

AMERICAN CHAPTERS

GRETA GORSUCH

WAYZGOOSE PRESS

Book design and editing by Maggie Sokolik, Wayzgoose Press

Cover Design by DJ Rogers, Book Branders

CONTENTS

SUMMER IN CIMARRON

LUNCH AT THE DIXIE DINER

SUMMER IN CIMARRON

CHAPTER ONE

Rhonda sat in her trailer. It was the same as every other day. She just sat in her trailer and looked out the window. There was not much to see. It was the same bare parking lot, same as yesterday and the day before. No trees. No flowers. No other people.

There were a few things Rhonda *could* see. She could see a big garbage dumpster. That wasn't so great. She could see the back of the Cimarron Highway Motel. It was a one-story building, maybe fifty years old. The motel was painted a light green on the front. The front faced Highway 64.

Rhonda's trailer was at the back of the motel. There the motel was a dirty white. Many years of sand and wind and snow had worked on the old paint. She could see a few patches of pink under the dirty white.

The owner of the Cimarron Highway Motel and Trailer Park, Mr. Mikey Sims, told Rhonda's brother Blue that the trailer park was a great place to stay for the summer.

"There are two parts to my business," he said. "The front

is the motel. It's on a busy street, Highway 64. But the back is our four-star trailer park. It's real quiet, you can't hear highway noise. It has everything your sister needs. Quiet, privacy. We have a shower house, and a place to wash clothes. And it's just $75 per week!"

Mr. Mikey Sims did not mention that the Cimarron Highway Motel and Trailer Park was on the wrong side of town. It was the side of town that no one went to. He also didn't mention that there had been no guests at the trailer park for over two years.

It took Blue five minutes to decide Rhonda's life. If he was going to a summer job in northern New Mexico, then Rhonda would stay nearby. They couldn't live together, of course. Blue would stay with his road crew. Rhonda would stay in Cimarron. It was a great place to spend the summer!

He picked out a four-star trailer park where she could stay, up in the mountains, with cool mornings. There were pine trees, and clear water. Lots of people wanted to live in Cimarron for the summer.

Rhonda had no words to say about this. Ever since her husband left her, she felt she had nothing to do. She didn't want to talk, or eat. She didn't care.

Blue, Rhonda's big brother, told her younger brother, "Well, OK. Let me take care of her for a while. We can't leave her like this. She lost her house. That husband of hers took all the money. She stopped going to work. Now she just sits around. So, I'll take her on, and then next year, you can take her."

Crosby, Rhonda's younger brother, said something that no one could hear. Blue and Crosby sighed. There was nothing else they could do. They didn't want to talk about it, really— not in front of Rhonda. She didn't care.

Now, Rhonda sat in a little trailer with no car, no tele-phone, and nothing to do. Blue left for his job, promising to come back on the weekend. As she looked out the window, she thought that the Cimarron Highway Motel and Trailer Park was more like a one-star place.

CHAPTER TWO

Crosby and Blue found a small, used trailer for Rhonda to stay in. There was not much to see inside the trailer. It had a small bed in the back. There was a small kitchen for cooking. There was a tiny icebox with fresh ice for milk and other cold foods.

Rhonda spent most of her time at the built-in table and chairs. They were blue and white, long ago. She could see out the window from there. There were some curtains in the windows. They were white-turned-yellow.

The trailer was pretty old. Someone used it for many years. Then, someone forgot it for many years. It probably sat in someone's back yard for months and months, out in the sun and rain. The inside smelled wet and cold. There was some dirt on the kitchen table. Rhonda could not see what color the floor was. *Maybe it was red and white*, she thought.

So, on her fourth morning at the Cimarron Highway Motel and Trailer Park, Rhonda woke up. She didn't like the smell of the trailer. She needed to open the windows and the door. It took her a few minutes to understand the trailer windows. They weren't like windows in a house that you just pulled up.

These windows wouldn't push to the side, either. To open the trailer windows Rhonda had to turn a handle. It took a long time. But if she kept on turning the handle, the window would open slowly. Then she had to go to the next window. She got most of the windows open. Then, she turned the handle of the door and opened it, too.

It was cold in Cimarron that morning. But, the air smelled sweet and fresh. For a minute, Rhonda forgot she was in a bare dirt parking lot no one ever visited. She forgot the big dumpster. She could almost smell… *what was it? Pine trees?* Having that fresh air in the trailer was a nice change. She turned around and went back to the small bed. She took everything off the bed and brought it outside. She wanted the fresh air smell where she slept, too.

Then, she looked at her icebox. She needed fresh ice if she wanted the milk to stay cold. She walked around to the front of the motel and walked in the door. An older woman sat behind the desk. She did not look up. Rhonda waited. The woman still did not look up.

"Excuse me," Rhonda said. Rhonda hadn't spoken for such a long time, she was almost surprised to hear herself. The older woman was surprised, too. She jumped and looked up.

"Oh," she said, in a high voice. "I didn't hear you come in." She turned off her mp3 player and took out her earbuds. "Can I help you?"

For a moment, Rhonda felt bad. She didn't want to talk to anyone. But, she needed ice. She had to think hard about what she wanted to say. Finally, she said in a quiet voice, "I'm Rhonda. I live in the trailer park."

"Oh, I heard about you. I'm Viv," the woman said. She didn't seem surprised it took Rhonda so long to answer. She smiled and stood up.

She was a big woman, and her bright purple dress made her look even larger. "I'm sorry I haven't walked back to see you. I have a little trouble walking. How are you doing?" Viv said.

Rhonda moved closer. She could see the woman's huge soft pink slippers. The lady's feet looked big and painful.

Viv continued, "It takes me a long time to get anywhere."

"Oh," Rhonda said. Then she said, "Well, it takes me a long time to say anything. So we're even."

Viv laughed. After a minute, Rhonda smiled a little. Then she said, in a small voice, "Do you have any ice? I need some for my icebox."

Viv gave Rhonda a small ice bucket and pointed to the ice machine outside the motel door. "Help yourself any time," she said.

Rhonda thanked her. She got a bucket of ice and returned to her little trailer. She poured it into her icebox. She felt tired, so she sat at her kitchen table. She felt the cool morning air move around inside her trailer.

The afternoon was a little warmer. It was early June in the little town. Rhonda was from Kansas. She was used to June being much warmer. Kansas was flat and had hot summers. When Blue and Rhonda first arrived in town, she noticed a sign that said:

Cimarron
Pop. 1,002
Elev. 6,430 feet (1,960 meters)

Cimarron was so high in the mountains, even June felt cold.

Rhonda walked out of the empty parking lot behind the motel, and looked up and down Highway 64. To the left, the west, she could see high mountains. *Was that snow on the mountains?* Rhonda looked closer. *Yes, it* was *snow.*

Viv waved from inside the motel office. Rhonda waved back. She didn't feel like talking much. She still felt sad that her husband left her. But Rhonda had also been alone for four days with nothing to do. She walked into the motel office.

"Did you find the ice machine?" Viv asked. She was doing something at her desk.

"Yes," Rhonda said. After a minute she said, "I only have an icebox. I can't keep much in it. Is there a store nearby? I don't have a car."

"Oh, sure," Viv said. "Do you know Cimarron at all?"

Rhonda shook her head.

"First timer? I thought so. We get a lot of tourists in summer. I don't always know everyone. But, I know who lives here year-round, and I was pretty sure I never saw you before." Viv looked at Rhonda.

Rhonda didn't know what to say, so she just said, "Uh-huh."

Viv stood up slowly. She got a large map and put it on the motel desk. "Let me tell you about Cimarron," she said.

She opened the map. Rhonda joined her at the desk. Both women looked down at the map. "Here is Highway 64." Viv drew her finger from left to right on the map. "And here we are." Viv pointed at a spot on Highway 64, right in the middle. Rhonda could see "Cimarron Highway Motel and Trailer Park" on the map.

Viv moved her hand over the part of town above Highway 64. "This is the north part of town," she said. "You cross Highway 64. Be careful, people drive too fast. Here is the city library. And here are some clothing shops. They're expensive. They're mostly for tourists. There's a nice bar here. It's open every night. A lot of year-round people go there to talk. And here is City Hall. And right there is the Cimarron post office."

Rhonda nodded her head. Everything looked close enough to walk. That was good. In fact, it looked like Rhonda could walk to most parts of town in ten minutes. Somehow, the idea felt exciting—a whole town to look at whenever she liked.

Viv moved her hand over the part of town under Highway 64. "This is the south part of town," she said. "This part of town is a little older." She pointed at a blue ribbon of water on the map. "This is the Cimarron River. It always has water in it, even in August. You cross the bridge and walk up the hill, and there's a big old hotel at the top. It has a restaurant. But, it's expensive."

"Is it for the tourists?" Rhonda asked, surprising herself.

"That's right!" Viv said, laughing. "Let's see." She pointed again. "Here is a museum for the town. The oldest house in town is there. It dates from 1850. Anyway, here you are. You can use it to get around."

No one had given Rhonda anything for a long time. Well, you could say that Blue gave her the trailer. But the map was like the key to a new chapter in an adventure story.

Rhonda walked back to her dirty trailer behind the Cimarron Highway Motel and Trailer Park. She stood with her map. She knew what to do.

CHAPTER FOUR

Using her map, Rhonda walked to the closest shop. It was only a few minutes away. She could see the sign that said, "One Stop Shop." She walked in. She was the only one in the shop.

A woman in her late thirties came from the back and said, "Hi, can I help you?" She had a nice smile.

"Oh… uh, hi," Rhonda said. "I'm staying at the trailer park and…"

"The trailer park? You mean behind the motel?" The woman seemed surprised.

"Yes, that's it. Anyway, I'm living in a used trailer. It really needs cleaning. What do you have for cleaning?" Rhonda asked.

"Oh, yes. We have some cleaning things," the woman said, moving to the front of the store. Together they picked out some soap, a blue bucket, and some window cleaner.

"The trailer doesn't smell very good. It smells wet, like there's water inside," Rhonda said. She didn't like saying it, but it was true.

The One Stop Shop woman picked up a small box. "Open this box," she said. "Then leave it in the spot that smells the worst." Then she went to the back of the store. "Here are some extra rags," she added. She handed Rhonda a bag filled with used clothes. "You can cut these up into cleaning rags."

"Oh no, I couldn't take that," Rhonda said.

"It's all right," the woman said. "My mother died a few months ago. She had clothes from forty years ago all over her house! She would like for someone to use these old clothes."

"Thank you," Rhonda said softly. She paid for the cleaning things. As she left the shop, she noticed a dusty box. The box said, "Christmas Lights, $5." She took the box to the woman. She asked, "Why is this only $5?"

"They're an old-type light. People want something newer when Christmas comes," the woman answered.

Rhonda paid her $5 and took the dusty box of Christmas lights with her.

"Do you know where I can buy milk?" Rhonda asked.

"Yes," the woman said. "Just walk five more minutes down Highway 64 and there's a grocery store." She added, "By the way, I'm Rosa. It's nice to meet you."

"I'm Rhonda. Well, thanks." Rhonda left and walked back to her trailer.

CHAPTER FIVE

Rhonda spent the whole afternoon cleaning the trailer. She pulled the mattress off the bed. She put it against the back wall of the motel, in the bright sunshine. She opened the small box she bought at the One Stop Shop and put it under the bed. She washed all the windows. Then, she started on the dirty floor.

After an hour, she could see the floor was red and white. It was pretty when it was clean. Rhonda washed the walls after that. They were a soft white. The small icebox was a bright brown wood. Under all that dirt, it looked great. The trailer started to look nice.

She opened the bag of rags Rosa gave her. Inside she found old t-shirts and a child's dress. She also found a set of curtains! They were bright white with red, blue, and green flowers. The curtains were old but they were clean. Rhonda could not believe her good luck. She took down the old white-turned-yellow curtains from the trailer and carried them to the dumpster. She put the new curtains up.

Rhonda heard a knock on the trailer door. "Yes?" she said.

It was Mr. Mikey Sims, the owner of the Cimarron Highway Motel and Trailer Park.

"Ah, yes, Mrs....?"

"My name's Rhonda," she said. She didn't want to hear the word "Mrs." It hurt too much.

"Yes. Right. My wife Viv sent me back here with these."

Rhonda went out to see. In the back of Mr. Sim's truck was a picnic table, two chairs, two big flower pots, and a box. Mr. Mikey Sims pulled everything out of the truck. He set up the picnic table and put the two chairs next to it. Then, he put the two flower pots next to Rhonda's trailer.

"If you just add water once or twice a week, some kind of plant will come up. I don't know what kind. Viv does all that," he said. Then, he handed her the box. "Viv said you might need some things for your house." He looked away. "If you need anything at all, please just ask."

Rhonda was so surprised she couldn't think of anything to say. The picnic table and chairs were new. It would be a great place to sit on warm days. She put the flower pots in the sun. She found her ice bucket, filled it with water, and then poured the water into the flower pots.

I wonder what they will be? she thought.

She took out the Christmas lights from the dusty box. She put the lights along the top of her trailer. At night, she could turn them on. It would look nice.

The empty parking lot at the back of the Cimarron Highway Motel and Trailer Park was dark at night. It was very, very dark, even though Highway 64 was close by. The motel blocked any light from the road.

Cimarron didn't have many street lights. At night, the whole town got dark. Rhonda liked it, but she would also like some colorful Christmas lights after it got dark. It was June, and not December, but it felt OK.

As the sun began to set, Rhonda moved her mattress back into the trailer. She took everything for the top of the bed inside. She made her bed. She closed a few of the windows. It was getting cold quickly.

She opened the box from Viv. Inside were books, colored pencils, paper, a coffee pot, two coffee cups, some sugar, two bowls, and forks, knives, and spoons. None of the forks, knives, and spoons matched. There were all different sizes and styles. Rhonda didn't mind. They looked fun, like they were all on an adventure together.

It was dark outside. Rhonda pulled the curtains closed. She went outside one last time and turned on her Christmas lights. They looked beautiful—blue, yellow, pink, red, green, and orange, all bright against the dark sky.

Sometime that night, Rhonda woke up suddenly. She heard something outside—something large. It moved slowly by her trailer. The Christmas lights were off. She couldn't see anything. It was quiet for a minute, and then she heard something by the dumpster. There was a loud bang and some noises. It was an animal noise, like crying. It was awful!

She heard a man yell, "Get out of there! Go on!"

Rhonda didn't know what to do. It was quiet again. After a while, she could see a light outside her trailer. There was a knock on her door.

"Who is it?" she said through the door. There was no way she going to open her door. She didn't know who—or what—was out there.

"Ma'am?" It was a man's voice. "I'm with the Cimarron police. Could you open the door?"

"Oh," Rhonda said. She opened the door.

The policeman said, "I'm Officer Garvey. Don't worry about anything, ma'am. We got a call that there was a bear back here. Sometimes the bears come to town at night. They smell food, and so they come to eat."

"A bear?" Rhonda said.

"Yes ma'am. We're very close to the mountains. This is bear country. They're hungry in early summer. No one really worries about them. It's important you don't leave any food out, and don't leave your pets outside. Do you have any pets? A dog or a cat?"

"No, no pets," Rhonda said.

Garvey said, "It's just a young black bear. He won't hurt anyone. But still, it's dark out there. We don't want anyone to run into him. Surprises are not good with bears."

Rhonda asked, "Is that a gun? You're not going to shoot him, are you?"

Garvey laughed. "Oh, no. This is a paintball gun. See?" He showed her the short little gun. It looked like a toy. Then, he pointed at the bright green paint balls that went into the gun. "It doesn't hurt him. It just surprises him, and gives him a bright green paint job on his fur."

Rhonda just looked at him. "Did that gun make the 'bang' sound I heard?" she asked.

"Yes ma'am. The gun makes a lot of noise. We don't want to hurt the bear, ma'am. Don't worry. We just have to teach him to look for food outside of Cimarron," Garvey said, finally.

"Well, thank you. Good night," Rhonda said, shutting the trailer door.

CHAPTER SEVEN

Rhonda woke up to a sunny, bright day. When she went outside she could not see the dumpster anymore. She went to ask Viv about it. Viv was not in the motel office, but Mr. Mikey Sims was.

"If you're looking for Viv, she's not here," he said.

"Oh," Rhonda said. "Is she OK?"

"Well," Mr. Sims said, "she went to the doctor today. She's not doing too well. Is there something I can help you with?"

"Oh, no, I just wanted to know what happened to the dumpster," Rhonda said.

Mr. Sims looked a little unhappy. He said, "Officer Garvey asked me to move the dumpster away from the trailer park. He thought that the bear came for the dumpster last night. He's worried that you might get scared."

Rhonda thought for a minute. She said, "Well I'm not so scared. But, I'd rather not be surprised by a bear, even a young one." She thought for another minute. "I'll stop by later to see how Viv is doing."

"All right, then," Mr. Mikey Sims replied. "She'd like that." He still looked unhappy.

Rhonda returned to her trailer. She kept the door open, and opened all the windows to let the cool, sunny air in. The trailer smelled better. It looked much better with the cleaning, too.

Rhonda kept thinking about the young black bear. She pictured it, crying, running away from town with bright green patches of paint on its coat.

She looked at the things Viv gave her yesterday. She picked up the paper and the colored pencils. She started to draw what she saw in her thoughts. After a few hours, she had a picture of the bear.

Rhonda didn't have breakfast. She felt hungry. She needed more ice for her icebox, milk, and some other groceries. Maybe she should buy some cheese or fruit.

She walked down Highway 64 to the small grocery store. She found the things she wanted: milk, bread, some cheese, and two apples. She also found some nice grapes, and bought those, too.

It was much warmer today. Strong winds were coming from the west, out of the mountains. All the snow was gone. Rhonda passed the One Stop Shop. She saw Rosa inside and stopped to say hello.

"There was a bear at the motel last night," she said.

"Oh, yes," Rosa said. "Garvey told me about him. He's just a young bear. I'm pretty sure I saw him a few nights ago. He's got a lot of green paint ball spots on him."

Both women laughed, but Rhonda thought the bear was a little sad, too. Then Rhonda said, "Thank you for the used clothes. There were some nice curtains in there. I used them in my trailer. My old curtains were so yellowed and dirty."

"You're welcome," Rosa said. "I help a lot of the older people in town. Their children grow up and then don't stay in Cimarron. So, the old people have lots of things in their houses, and no one to give them to. When I ask, they give me their old things. I give them to other people who need them. We have some families with kids in town. Our schools are good. But there aren't many paying jobs in Cimarron. A lot of mothers and fathers drive forty miles away to work. No one has a lot of money, really."

"Wow," Rhonda said. She didn't have anything to say.

CHAPTER EIGHT

Rhonda got home and made lunch. She took her picture of the running bear to give to Viv. Viv was at home, but she was lying down. She didn't look well. This worried Rhonda. Rhonda sat with her awhile. Viv was always so nice to her.

"Is there anything I can do to help?" Rhonda asked.

"Well," Viv said. "I could use some books. Have you been to the Cimarron library yet?"

"No, not yet," Rhonda said. "But I can find it on the map. Is it open today?"

Viv said, "It should be. But be careful. You'll have to cross Highway 64. It's a busy road."

Rhonda went to the library. It was small and in an old building. This was a new part of Cimarron for her. The streets were newer, and ran straight from east to west and north to south. There were a lot of small, older homes. The library was an old business building. It had a high front with large windows. When Rhonda went inside, the front room was bright, and full of books.

"Hi, can I help you?" the librarian asked. He was an older man with white hair.

"Yes, uh... hello," Rhonda said. She felt shy talking to people. But she knew Viv now, and Rosa. And, Viv needed some books to read.

"I'm here to get some books for my friend," she said.

"Yes?" the librarian said. He waited.

"I think she likes history books and mysteries," Rhonda said.

"Oh, we have some good ones," the librarian said. "We have our new books over there." He walked over to a table with books on it. "What about you? What do you like to read?"

Rhonda was surprised by the question. No one asked her that question before, especially her husband. She thought about it.

"I like art books. I can't draw very well, but I like to get ideas. Sometimes I paint things in my house," she said. Then she thought, *Well... I used to. I don't have a house anymore.* She felt sad, but she kept talking.

"Do you have any art books?" Rhonda asked.

"I'm sure we do," the librarian said. "First, let's get you a library card. Then, you can borrow books."

Before she left the library, Rhonda went to the computers in the back. The computers were connected to the internet. Library guests could use them for up to twenty minutes.

Rhonda didn't really use computers. Her husband had one, but he wouldn't let her use it. That was how he met his new girlfriend—he found love on the internet. That was why he left Rhonda.

Was that true? Rhonda thought. *Wouldn't he leave me anyway?*

Rhonda suddenly felt so sad she could not think. She felt like crying.

After a minute, she looked at the computer. She told herself she didn't care anymore. She needed to use the computer, and the library had one.

She typed in her brother Blue's e-mail address. He might be checking his e-mail. She wrote:

> I'm fine. I'm at the library. How are you? Are you coming to Cimarron this weekend?

He answered right away. He wrote:

> Good to hear from you. Yes, I'll be there on Saturday. Around 9 AM? Do you need anything?

She answered:

> Yes. Could you bring me some small cans of paint and some very small paint brushes? Just blue, brown, green, and red? Maybe some purple? And white?

Blue answered:

> Of course. Anything, dear sister. I have to go. Someone from the road crew is calling.
>
> Love, Blue

Back at the Cimarron Highway Motel and Trailer Park, Rhonda dropped off Viv's books. Viv was still lying down, but she looked better. Her face had more color.

Rhonda went to her trailer. She looked at the two art books she found at the library. One of the books was about art in New Mexico. Rhonda loved it. There were sunsets, mountains, pine trees, and animals. One of the paintings was of a bear. She spent a few hours drawing another picture of the young black bear, running out of town. She used some ideas from the art book and added more color around the bear.

The second art book had very small letters. It showed Japanese and Chinese art. Rhonda wanted to read what the book said. She didn't know very much about art from Japan and China. Rhonda tried holding the book close to her eyes. She still couldn't read the words.

Rhonda wondered if she needed reading glasses. She was 47. Her age was right for reading glasses. She sighed. It was Friday. She didn't have much money until Blue came.

It was still bright outside, and much warmer. Rhonda felt like taking a walk. She went a different direction this time, using her map of Cimarron. She walked west, past the One Stop Shop. Then, she turned left on a small road. The road became even smaller. There was tall green grass on all sides. The road took her to the Cimarron River.

The river was running fast. It made a noise like laughter. Rhonda could see all the way to the bottom, the water was really clear. She couldn't see Highway 64, she couldn't hear it. She didn't see houses or buildings.

She heard a sound. She froze. There was a black bear less than twenty feet away! It was the young one. She knew this because there was bright green paint all over his coat. The bear found a large silver fish and was eating it. He didn't see Rhonda.

She wasn't scared, but she remembered what Garvey said, "Surprises are not good with bears." She walked back, very slowly, until she came to Highway 64. Then, she turned back to town and walked fast. She didn't want to tell anyone she saw the bear. If she left the bear alone, it would leave her alone.

She walked past the One Stop Shop again. Rosa waved hello from inside, waving her hand for Rhonda to come in.

"What happened? Did something scare you?" Rosa asked. "You're breathing hard."

"Oh, it was nothing. I'm not used to Cimarron's being 6000 feet high yet!" Rhonda said.

"6,430 feet! Yeah, that'll take another week or so," Rosa said. "Anyway, I asked you in to show you something." She took out a large flat box. It was tied with a beautiful blue ribbon. Inside the box were fifty or more pairs of reading glasses! There were men's glasses, women's glasses, and children's glasses. They were all shapes, colors, and sizes. Some seemed old, and many seemed new, as if they were never used.

"Oh," Rhonda said. "Oh…"

"I know," Rosa said. "Aren't they wonderful? An old woman gave them to me. She was cleaning out her house. She never threw anything away."

"May I… may I see a pair?" Rhonda said. She picked up a pair of black glasses and slipped them on. Then she picked up a book. She could see the pages perfectly!

"I would like to buy this pair," she said.

"Oh no, just take them," Rosa said, shaking her head. "I have no idea what to do with these."

Rhonda had an idea what to do with the glasses.

CHAPTER TEN

When Blue arrived the next morning in his truck, he found Rhonda outside at the picnic table. She was drinking a cup of coffee. She was also cleaning a pair of black glasses. They looked brand new, and flashed in the sunlight.

Rhonda looked up and smiled. She stood up. "How are you?" she said.

Blue was very shocked. The week before, he left Rhonda sitting in an old trailer. She didn't talk, she didn't eat. She didn't wash her hair. Now she was smiling and talking. Her clothes were clean, and her face had good color. *Did she get a little sun this week?* Blue wondered. He could not believe the change in her.

"How's work?" she asked.

"Pretty good," he said. "I have a good road crew this year. I might be done in July."

"Oh," she said. She wasn't sure what she would do if he left New Mexico. "Well, OK," she said, finally. Then she asked, "Did you bring the paint and the little paint brushes?"

He nodded, and got them from the truck for her. She was

like a child opening presents at Christmas. She held up the different bottles of paint and looked at the paint brushes. She lined them up on the picnic table.

"Thank you!" she said. "Thank you, thank you, thank you!"

Blue got some coffee from the trailer, and they sat and talked. Rhonda told Blue about the people she met. She told him how she cleaned up the trailer. She told him about the bear. She told him about her walks in Cimarron.

"So you like it here," Blue said.

"Yes, for now," she said. "I hear that tourists start coming around this time of year. It's getting warmer. It might seem different with so many cars and people."

"Yeah, maybe," he said.

He gave her some money and a bag of groceries. He also gave her a cell phone. It had earbuds she could use. "You can use this to call me. There's some music on it, too. You can use it like an mp3 player," he said. He could see she looked unhappy. "What is it?" he asked.

Rhonda gave a big sigh. "I don't like taking money from you. I love you, you're my brother, but... I've been thinking... I want to find that husband of mine," she said.

Blue froze. "No!" he said. He was shocked again, but in a bad way. "He's no good. Why do you want to find him?"

"Oh, I don't want to be with him," she said. "Don't worry about that. He broke my heart. He found love somewhere else. But... I... want... my... MONEY. Half of that money was mine. He took it all. I want my half."

Blue smiled, and then he laughed. "Oh, good one," he said, finally. "All right, then. Let me call Crosby. It might take some time to find that no-good husband of yours. Crosby might find him. When my job is done in July, we'll go and get your money."

Rhonda smiled with all her white teeth. Maybe she lived on the wrong side of town in her little trailer, but now she felt like she lived on the right side of her life.

CHAPTER ELEVEN

Rhonda spent Sunday painting her new reading glasses. After she cleaned them, she thought she could add some art to the sides. The glasses were a plain black. She thought some color would make them prettier. She added flowers and grasses. Finally, she used brown paint to show a very small bear with even smaller green patches on his coat. That design was just over the right eye of the glasses.

She let them dry, and then tried them on. Looking in the mirror inside her trailer, her mouth opened. She couldn't believe it. They looked great! The glasses were pretty, and interesting. She thought some more, and planned a trip back to the One Stop Shop on Monday.

Cold weather came in from the mountains. She could see black clouds to the west. The wind picked up. Some trees near the trailer park moved in the wind. That night, Rhonda could hear the rain shower down on the top of her trailer.

The next day was cold but clear. Sure enough, the tourists came. Suddenly, there were twice as many cars and trailers. Some trailers were really big. Rhonda saw groups of people at the restaurants across Highway 64. There were even a few cars in front of the Cimarron Highway Motel and Trailer Park. Mr. Mikey Sims had guests.

As Rhonda left the trailer park to visit the One Stop Shop, she saw a huge, new trailer slowing down in front of the motel. The trailer pulled over and the driver got out. He didn't say hello. He went into the motel. A minute later Mr. Mikey Sims walked with the man back to the trailer park, where Rhonda's trailer was.

Just a few seconds later, the driver came back to the truck, walking fast. He shook his head "no," got into his truck, and pulled away. Mr. Sims stood there, watching the trailer leave. Mr. Sims shook his head, and walked back into the motel office. It looked as though Rhonda would still have some privacy in the trailer park.

Huh, Rhonda thought. *Maybe they didn't like the bare dirt parking lot? Or my little trailer?* She laughed, and then walked to the One Stop Shop.

There were a lot of people in the store. They looked like tourists. It was still cold outside from the rain, but they weren't wearing jackets. Two of the women complained about the cold to Rosa. One said, "It's June, why is it still so cold here?" Rosa said something about Cimarron being at 6,430 feet. Some people bought bright yellow "New Mexico" jackets. Others bought sweaters. One little boy found a hat he wanted.

When Rosa finally had time, she came to Rhonda.

"Whew," she said. "Tourist season has begun!" Rhonda and Rosa laughed together. The tourists were good for business, but they weren't fun.

"What's up?" Rosa asked. Rhonda showed Rosa her painted glasses. Rosa said, "What? No way! These look great! How did you do that?"

Rhonda told how she cleaned the glasses, and how she got the idea for the art on the sides. She told Rosa she wanted to buy the box of glasses. She wanted to make some more "art reading glasses."

Rosa sold the glasses to her at a low price. She told Rhonda she would help her sell them at the One Stop Shop. She added, "You might give a few pairs to the library. People always need glasses there. The tourists will see them, too. Some of them stop at the library to use the computers. You can't get good internet up here. The library has good internet, though."

Rhonda thanked Rosa and walked home with the box of old reading glasses.

CHAPTER TWELVE

After a week, Rhonda cleaned and painted twenty pairs of glasses. She took some of the glasses to the One Stop Shop. The others she took to the library as a gift. "If anyone asks about them," Rhonda said, "just tell them the One Stop Shop has more!"

"Thanks," the librarian said. He told her he would give people the message.

The men's glasses had bears, horses, cars, trees, fish, and grass on them. Their colors were darker. The women's glasses had flowers and grass, and brighter colors. The women's glasses always had the little black bear, running away, with green spots on his coat.

Rhonda used ideas from her art books. She even got some ideas from Viv. When she visited the motel office, Viv was sitting up. Viv told her some stories about Cimarron. She told Rhonda that Cimarron was Spanish for "wild horse." Rhonda wasn't sure why the town was named for wild horses.

Viv told Rhonda that when her grandparents came to Cimarron, no one had cars. They used horses. "This was many years ago," she said. "Cimarron also had a wild bar. Rough men would come to the bar and shoot their guns. Then they would get chased out of town."

Just like that young black bear, Rhonda thought.

After two more weeks, Rhonda sold almost all her glasses. Rosa was happy. They both made good money. She promised to find Rhonda some more used glasses. Rhonda also called Blue on her cell phone. She wanted to visit the towns around Cimarron. She hoped to find more used glasses at some churches or used clothing shops. She could also ask tourist shops if they wanted to sell her "art reading glasses." She wanted to use his truck.

Blue was surprised, but said OK. He took an extra day off work, and they visited three towns in northern New Mexico. They found sixty pairs of glasses for free or very low prices.

No one could understand why someone would want old reading glasses. There was something sad about them. Their owners were gone. No one wanted them anymore. *Hmmm,* Rhonda thought. *And now they can have new owners. Someone else will want them.*

On their way back to Cimarron, Blue said that their younger brother Crosby found Rhonda's "no-good husband." He was still in Kansas. "Do you still want to see him?" he asked.

Rhonda was quiet for a few minutes. Then she said, "Yes. I want my half of the money."

"OK," Blue said. "Two more weeks and my job is done. Then we can go." They had a plan.

CHAPTER THIRTEEN

The day came when it was time to leave. Rhonda took thirty more pairs of glasses to the One Stop Shop. She had thirty more to take to the other towns to sell. However, that would come later.

Rosa looked at the art on one pair of glasses. "This is new," she said, pointing at the tiny building painted on the side of the glasses.

"Yes," Rhonda said. "Each of those glasses has something from Cimarron. I got ideas for the art from my walks."

As they talked, an older man asked to see a pair of glasses with a tiny Cimarron library painted on them. He tried them on and bought them in about ten seconds.

"So," Rosa asked, "are we going to see you again?"

"Yes," Rhonda said. "I'll be gone just a week. Then I'll come back, and... who knows? I'll find something else to do."

The two women said goodbye.

Rhonda's trailer was hitched to Blue's truck. All the windows were closed. The trailer was ready to travel down Highway 64. They would meet Crosby, and get her money from... Donald... there, she said his name in her head. Donald, her no-good husband.

When Rhonda returned to Cimarron, she would have her own truck. She could pull the trailer herself. She already told Mr. Mikey Sims goodbye. He asked if she might come back to the trailer park. She answered, "I don't know. I'd like more flowers and trees. It's also too dark back there."

"Oh," Mr. Sims said.

"And, it's going to get cold in Cimarron when the winter season starts," Rhonda said.

"That's true," he said. "But you know, Viv has some ideas about that. We have a place on the side of the motel. The trailer would be protected from the snow there. We could find a way to keep your trailer warm and dry. Maybe I can find a few trees and plant them in the trailer park, too."

Rhonda waited. Then she said, "OK, we'll talk about it when I get back."

Mr. Mikey Sims smiled—or at least he didn't look unhappy.

They got into Blue's truck. As the truck slowly pulled away, Rhonda saw something interesting. On the white painted side of the Cimarron Highway Motel and Trailer Park building, she saw some big patches of fresh, bright green paint. The young black bear was back. Then Rhonda knew she would be back, too. After all, it would still be summer in Cimarron.

LUNCH AT THE DIXIE DINER

CHAPTER ONE
NURSE ANDREA

Andrea was washing her truck. She was in front of her house with a bucket and the water hose. She was doing her best to wash the dust and road oil off the truck. It was harder work than most people thought. You had to wash and work at it—use more soap from the bucket, then more water, then more soap.

She checked her watch. It was 10:30 in the morning. She still had time to finish washing her old red truck, and change her clothes. Andrea needed to pick up her mother to take her to lunch at 11:30. There was still an hour to go.

Andrea sighed. The idea of picking up her mother at the Fairfield Nursing Home made her feel tired. Andrea was a night nurse at a large hospital about an hour away. There wasn't any work in her small town of Fairfield, Texas, except for the Fairfield Nursing Home. The nursing home took in the old and sick people of the area—people who couldn't take care of themselves.

Andrea's home town was in a farming area. There weren't many people there, and there weren't many businesses. People didn't spend a lot of money. The Fairfield Nursing Home was not looking for nurses or other workers. Andrea called them twice a year, but there were never any new jobs. Anyway, she wasn't sure she wanted to work in the same place her mother was living. She loved her mother, and she felt bad she had to live at the Fairfield Nursing Home.

Andrea liked her hospital job, but she had to work at night, and it was over an hour away. She left for work at 9:30 each evening.

Every night, she got a cup of coffee at the Dixie Diner. She carried it out to her truck and drove to her job through the darkness. She got to the hospital around 10:30. She had to be at her desk on the third floor at 11:00. Then, she worked all night until 7:00 in the morning. Some nights were long and quiet. Other nights were busy. It was a hospital. You never knew what would happen.

Every morning, she went home the same way. She drove her truck through the new, sunny day. Sometimes she would sleep for a few hours. Once a week, she picked up her mother and took her to lunch. This was one of those mornings.

Andrea got home from work and slept a few hours. Now, she was up. She wore old clothes so she could wash her truck. She had on some old blue jeans and an old blue t-shirt. They were soft, and she loved them.

It was getting hot and sunny. Andrea kept washing her old truck, and it started to look a little better. Her telephone rang. She quickly dried her hands off and reached for her phone.

"Hello?" Andrea said.

"Andrea?"

"Yeah. Tiffany?"

"Hey, good morning. What's up?" Tiffany said.

"Oh, you know. Work was long. I got home around 8."

"Oh yeah? Good. Well, I have some news."

"OK." There was a silence.

Tiffany said, "The Fairfield Nursing Home is looking for some new people. They have some jobs!"

"Oh?" There was more silence.

"You don't sound too happy about it."

"What?" Andrea said. "No, no, it's interesting news."

Tiffany, who was Andrea's oldest friend, laughed. Then she said "Well, if that is how you show interest, I would hate to see how you show you're *not* interested."

Andrea said, "I'm just still a little tired."

Finally Tiffany said, "Are you taking your mother to lunch today?"

Surprised, Andrea said, "How did you know?"

Tiffany laughed a little and said, "Oh, I just made a guess."

Andrea laughed, too, and said, "You guessed right. I have to go now and change my clothes. Are you working tomorrow?" Tiffany was a cook at the Fairfield Nursing Home.

"No! I have the day off. Let's meet up. Maybe for coffee?"

"Yeah. Sounds good!"

"Now that's showing interest. Where should we meet?"

Andrea laughed hard. There was only one place to get coffee in Fairfield. That was at the Dixie Diner.

"Oh, you. See you at the diner around... 9 in the morning?"

Tiffany laughed back and said, "I think I can get there."

The two friends said goodbye. Andrea looked at her watch. It was already 11:20. She had to leave right away. She didn't have time to change her clothes. They had soap and water all over them. There was even some road oil on her blue jeans. There was nothing she could do about it now.

She jumped into her truck, started it, and drove down her street. She left the bucket and the water hose in front of her little house.

Her street was lined with little houses, a few trees, and a lot of yellow and brown grass. Fairfield, Texas needed rain. Rain didn't happen often enough in that part of the country.

Andrea looked at her watch again and knew she would be late.

CHAPTER THREE
MILEY

Miley sat in the easy chair near the door. She was an 85-year-old woman. She had short white hair and blue eyes that looked large behind her big, bright blue-rimmed glasses. She remembered picking the glasses out, but when was it? Last week? She couldn't remember. She was with someone at the time. She couldn't remember who.

Miley loved those glasses. She wasn't small. She was short but wide. She could move fast if she needed to. That often surprised people.

Miley was Andrea's mother. Although Miley didn't think of that. She was hungry, and she had the feeling something was going to happen. She couldn't remember how it happened but she was sitting near the door with dark blue pants, soft shoes, and a white shirt. And, her blue-rimmed glasses, of course. The sun caught them and flashed. Miley smiled at that.

Who was coming? What was she waiting for? She checked her bag. She had a little money and a few other things. She was ready. She was also hungry. She was just standing up to have lunch when the sun flashed off the front of an old red truck. The truck pulled to the front of the Fairfield Nursing Home and stopped. Miley knew the truck had something to do with her.

Miley saw a blonde woman with blue jeans get out of the truck and come to the front door.

"Mom!" she said.

Miley smiled. The woman looked like Miley should go with her. She stepped to the door, and then stopped. She asked, "Where are we going?"

Andrea said, "Sorry I'm late, Mom!"

Miley asked again, "Where are we going?"

Andrea answered, "Well, there's a new fried chicken place we can try."

Miley answered by walking out the door to the red truck. She got into the truck slowly. The truck was high and Miley had to climb up. The woman in the blue jeans and dirty blue t-shirt was behind her. Miley wouldn't fall.

"Here, Mom" she said, handing Miley her bag.

Andrea started the truck and they rolled out to the bright and dusty road in front of the nursing home.

Miley said, "How do I know you?"

The woman looked away. She was brushing some dirt off of her t-shirt. "Well Mom, I'm your daughter."

Miley put her head to one side and thought about this. There was a silence. Then she said, "Are we going to lunch? I'm hungry."

The woman answered, "Yes. Does fried chicken sound OK to you?"

Miley said, "Andrea."

Andrea answered, "Yes."

CHAPTER FOUR
JOHN HARPER

On the way to the fried chicken restaurant, Andrea passed three large, new-looking trucks. They were all blue and really huge. They had "Harper Brothers Trucking, Dallas Texas" painted on their sides. Each of them had eighteen wheels.

The drivers were professional truck drivers, and it looked like they had been driving for many hours. One of the trucks was going very slowly. It looked like something was wrong. Andrea could see that two of the eighteen wheels were flat. Andrea shook her head. Miley put her head to one side and reached into her bag.

Andrea saw the fried chicken restaurant and turned into the parking lot. She stopped her truck and got out. She walked to the other door to help Miley out. She saw her mother write something on a piece of paper.

"What are you doing, Mom?" she asked.

Miley answered, "Oh just a little note." Then she smiled. The bright sun flashed off her glasses.

Andrea got Miley out of the truck and went to the fried

chicken place. But the windows were dark, and it was closed. Andrea knocked on the glass door but no one came.

Andrea said, "I think they're closed, Mom. That leaves Dixie Diner. Are you OK with that?"

Miley answered "That's OK. Do they have coffee?"

"Coffee?"

"I haven't had coffee for such a long time," Miley said.

"Mom, didn't you have coffee this morning at breakfast? At the nursing home?" Andrea asked.

There was a short silence. "That's not very good coffee," Andrea's mother said. "I can see the bottom of the cup through the coffee."

Andrea made a face and laughed. The Dixie Diner wasn't far away. Fairfield, Texas was a small town. She thought they could walk to the diner. She took Miley's arm and they slowly walked down the road.

"Is it OK if we walk, Mom?" Andrea asked. Her mother did not answer. She was holding the piece of paper in her hand. Andrea moved to take the paper but Miley moved quickly away. This surprised Andrea, but then she remembered how fast her mother could move when she wanted to.

Andrea said, "I don't want you to lose your paper."

"Don't you worry about this paper. I'm holding on to it. Do they have coffee, where we're going?" her mother answered.

Andrea said, "Yes, they have coffee. I buy it every night before work."

"Oh good," her mother said.

As they walked to the diner, the three large blue trucks passed them. They were still moving slowly, one after the other. Andrea could see them pull over to the diner. The three drivers got out and talked in a group. One man's voice was louder than the others'.

"We have to do something here. We can't wait until we get to Dallas!"

The other two men talked in softer voices. The second man said, "There's nothing here in this town. We have to try to get to Dallas for those wheels."

Andrea and Miley walked around the men to get to the Dixie Diner.

Andrea walked over and spoke to the tallest man. "Hi. Looks like you had some trouble," she said.

"Yes, we have two flats. And we're short on time. We have to get to Dallas," he said. He had dark hair and deep lines around his eyes. He looked around forty. He seemed tired, but friendly, like he thought the world was a good place. His brown shirt had his name on it, "John Harper."

Andrea said, "There's a good garage down the street. I'm not sure, but I think they can fix large wheels like that. It's a small place, but the owner is fair. He does good work." Andrea pointed to a small building down the road.

"Thanks," the man named John Harper said. He turned to the other two men. "Let's go in and get something to eat. Then we can check on that shop."

The men nodded. As Andrea and Miley moved to the diner door, John Harper moved quickly ahead and opened the door for them. "Thank you," Andrea said. Miley smiled.

CHAPTER FIVE
TRUCKING BUSINESS

Andrea found a table for two in the diner. Her mother moved very slowly, smiling at people she knew. She talked to a few. To one older man she said, "I'm just here for the coffee. This nice lady is taking me out." She pointed at her daughter.

"Come on, Mom. Here's a nice table," Andrea said. Finally, after a long, long time, Miley sat down.

"I'll be back, Mom. I need to clean up a little." Miley put her head to one side.

Andrea went to the restroom in back and splashed water on her face. She tried to brush some of the road oil and dirt off of her t-shirt and blue jeans. It only took a minute. She came out of the restroom and could not see her mother.

She could see her purse. Andrea picked up her mother's bag and looked around the diner. When she walked to the front of the diner, near the door, she saw her mother sitting at a large table with the three truck drivers. *What?* Andrea thought.

She moved quickly to the table. "Mom? What are you doing?" She looked at John Harper and his two brothers. "I'm sorry. We're just out for lunch. Mom gets a little lost sometimes."

Her mother started talking at the same time. She said, "Do you think we could get some good coffee here? I haven't had good coffee for such a long time." And she looked around for the waitress. The waitress came by with five glasses of water. She pulled up another chair for Andrea.

Miley asked the waitress for coffee. Andrea and the men also asked for coffee. Andrea didn't know what else to do. The truck drivers didn't seem unhappy that her mother sat down with them. In fact, the other two men started talking to Miley and Andrea. They said their names were Al and Michael. They were Harpers, too.

Al said, "I'm the oldest, John here is the middle brother, and Michael is the baby of the family."

Michael laughed. He was short, and had dark hair. He had a brown shirt like John's that said, "Michael Harper." The three men were the Harper Brothers. They owned the three large blue trucks. They talked about their trucking business. They drove six days a week, and sometimes even seven. They drove from Dallas to all other cities in Texas.

Their coffee arrived, and everyone ordered something to eat. Andrea had really wanted fried chicken. She was unhappy that the fried chicken place was closed, so she ordered some fried chicken and salad. John Harper ordered fried chicken, too. Miley smiled and looked from John Harper to Andrea.

John started talking to Andrea. He asked if she was from Fairfield. She said she was. She said, "There aren't any jobs here. So I work at night as a nurse about an hour away."

John Harper asked if her job was interesting. Andrea said, "Sometimes. Mostly it's very quiet. It's a hospital. People are sleeping. I get pretty good money for it."

John and his brothers talked about their business, and how Texas needed more rain. Their father had been a farmer. It was hard to do well when it didn't rain. When he died, they took the money he left them and started their trucking business.

Andrea agreed about the rain. Everything was dusty and brown.

CHAPTER SIX
GOING TO RAIN

"Mom, we need to be going back," Andrea said. "I've got to get some more sleep. I'm working tonight."

Miley didn't answer, but got up. She smiled at the three Harpers. A piece of paper fell to the table.

John Harper picked it up and said, "You dropped this." Miley's blue-rimmed glasses flashed in the sunlight coming in the window.

"That's not mine. I'm sure it's yours now," she said. She moved slowly to the front door of the Dixie Diner. Andrea followed, and said goodbye to the three Harper brothers.

"The garage you want is right down there. Good luck," she said. The men waved goodbye.

Miley said, "I think you should go out with John Harper."

Andrea was surprised. "What? Where did you get that idea?" she said. She looked down at her dirty blue t-shirt and blue jeans.

Andrea was not young anymore. She had been a nurse for twenty years. She had worked hard. She was about forty. She wasn't pretty, but she wasn't bad looking. And today, her clothes were not right for going out, even to the Dixie Diner.

Her hair was dark blonde, almost brown, and medium length. She hadn't washed it this morning. Her friend Tiffany had long beautiful blonde hair. Tiffany was always telling Andrea to grow her hair longer, and take better care of it. But, Andrea was busy with her work. She never thought about it. The idea that a man like John Harper would be interested in her was funny.

She laughed, and her mother laughed with her. The wind picked up on their way back to the old red truck. It was cooling off, but there was dust on Andrea's truck. *Even after all that washing,* Andrea thought.

"It's going to rain," Miley said.

"I would like that," answered her daughter.

CHAPTER SEVEN
IS THERE A JOB?

There wasn't any rain the next day, or the next. A few more days went by. Andrea took the hose and watered the brown grass in front of her house. She drove to the hospital at 9:30 every night with her cup of coffee. In the morning, she drove back home in the morning sun. It was a little cooler. There wasn't as much dust.

She met her friend Tiffany twice for coffee. Each time, Tiffany told her that the Fairfield Nursing Home needed a nurse, and that she should go in and ask about the job. Andrea said she would.

The next day, Andrea stopped at the Dixie Diner on the way home from work. She got two cups of coffee. She carried the coffee to her truck and drove to the Fairfield Nursing Home. She found Miley in a sunny room with a few other old women.

"Hi, Mom. I brought some coffee." She handed the cup to her mother, who smiled and drank it all in less than a minute.

Andrea sat down. She was a little surprised. The coffee was

hot. Then she handed her coffee to her mother, and Miley drank that down, too. Her blue-rimmed eye glasses flashed.

"It's going to rain tonight," Miley said.

Andrea smiled at that. She hoped it would, too. Then Andrea kissed her mother and walked into the main office of the Fairfield Nursing Home. She asked about the nursing job.

On her last night at the hospital, Andrea walked to each room on the third floor. Everyone was asleep. There were no surprises that night. Andrea noticed it was raining—hard. She could see out the window into the darkness. Rain was coming down. An hour later, it was still raining.

Andrea said goodbye to her friends at the hospital. It was her last day. She had taken the job at the Fairfield Nursing Home. She would still work at night, but she could drive to the nursing home in only ten minutes. The money was good.

First, she would take a week off and maybe visit Dallas. Then, she would start her new job.

By the time Andrea got to her truck in the hospital parking lot, the rain had stopped. The morning was dark and gray. The air smelled good. She drove toward home. About half way there, she could see the sun coming through the clouds. She pulled over to the side of the road to rest, and watch the sun come out.

It was beautiful, and the air was cool. She didn't see the

really huge blue truck pass. It slowed down and then stopped, its lights flashing.

Andrea was surprised to see a tall, dark-haired man get out of the truck and walk toward her. He waved and smiled. It was John Harper. Andrea felt very warm.

When he reached her old red truck, she asked him, "How did you know it was me?"

He smiled and showed her a piece of paper, the one Miley had dropped on the table at the Dixie Diner. It said:

Andrea
Lunch at the Dixie Diner
Texas BXN 1414

"Texas BXN 1414 is the license number on your truck," John Harper said. "I've been looking for you." He smiled.

Andrea smiled back, and together they watched the new sun come up.

BOOKS IN THIS SERIES

American Chapters books by Greta Gorsuch